nickelodeon

DORA
and Friends

The PRINCESS and the RING

Adapted by Mary Tillworth

Based on the teleplay "The Magic Ring"
by Valerie Walsh Valdes

Illustrated by Marilena Perilli and Victoria Miller

A GOLDEN BOOK • NEW YORK

T#: 306096
randomhousekids.com
ISBN 978-0-553-49768-7
Printed in the United States of America
10 9 8 7 6 5 4 3 2 1

One day, Dora and Naiya were leaving a kindergarten class after reading the children a story about ancient treasure. Suddenly, Pablo rushed up to them. He had found a beautiful gold ring!

Naiya admired it. "That looks like the ancient treasure from our story!"

"Cool!" said Pablo. He slipped the ring on his finger.

There was a puff of smoke.

Dora and Naiya looked around. Pablo had disappeared!

"Down here!" called Pablo. He had shrunk!

"There must have been a spell on the ring!" said Naiya.

Pablo was worried. "I can't stay this size. I'm supposed to have story time with the kids!"

Dora crouched down. "*No te preocupes, Pablo.* We'll figure out how to break the spell so you can be big again."

Naiya studied the ring. "Let's go to the library. I bet we can find out where this ring came from."

In the library, the three friends found a book that showed a picture of Pablo's ring. They learned that the ring had been a special present to a princess from her mother. A spell protected the magic ring. If anyone other than the princess wore it, he or she would shrink!

   One day, a greedy wizard who worked for
the princess stole the ring. A little mouse
named Mousey saw the wizard put it on and
shrink! The wizard was so tiny, he dropped the
ring and lost it.

   "'The spell cannot be broken until whoever
has the ring puts it on the finger of the
princess,'" read Dora.

   "Pablo, can you show us where you found
the ring?" asked Naiya.

Pablo led them to a city garden. Next to it was a very old wall. When Dora held the ring up to the wall, a tiny door appeared. It was a doorway to the princess's world!

But when Pablo tried to take the ring through the door, it was too big for him to carry by himself!

"We've all got to shrink so we can help you return the ring!" said Dora. She put the ring on, and she shrank, too.

Naiya put the ring on next. *Poof!* Now all three friends were ready for their big adventure. They picked up the ring and went through the doorway.

Dora, Naiya, and Pablo found themselves on the busy streets of an ancient city.

"Wow, everything looks so big!" Pablo said.
He started to walk down the middle of the street.

Dora pulled him back. "We can't be seen
so small—someone will think we've stolen the
ring from the princess." She spotted a mouse
hole. "We can hide in there. C'mon!"

Inside the mouse hole, the three friends met Mousey from the story of the princess and the ring! Mousey offered them a ride to the palace to return the ring to the princess.

"We have to watch out for the wizard and his cat—they're looking for the ring," Mousey warned as they set off.

As Dora and her friends traveled through the city streets, the wizard spotted them. He started to chase them!

Mousey turned a corner and lost the wizard. But he was going so fast, the ring went flying.

It landed on the edge of a seesaw. Two men moved the seesaw, and the ring flew into the air again!

"Catch it, catch it, catch it!" called Dora. She and her friends held their hands up . . . and caught the ring!

With the ring safe, Mousey raced to the royal palace.

When they arrived, Mousey led them to the princess's bedroom. The princess was taking a nap.

"How are we gonna get up there?" asked Pablo, staring at the huge bed.

Naiya spotted a teacup and a spoon on a table next to the bed. "We can make a seesaw!"

The friends climbed onto the table and balanced the spoon on the teacup. Then Mousey scurried up and jumped onto the spoon, catapulting them right onto the princess's pillow!

Dora, Naiya, and Pablo went over to slip the ring onto the princess's finger. Suddenly, the wizard's cat jumped onto the bed. The tiny wizard leapt off his cat and put his hand on the ring, too!

The princess woke up just as everyone
turned big again.

"Princess! These are the thieves who stole
your ring!" declared the wizard.

"No, Your Highness! The wizard took the
ring!" said Dora.

The princess shook her head. "He's my royal
wizard—he wouldn't do that." She called the
palace guards.

As the guards were taking Dora and her friends away, Mousey jumped in front of the princess. The princess threw up her hands in surprise—and the ring flew off!

Mousey picked up the ring and
ran out of the room. The princess,
the guards, the wizard and his cat, and
Dora and her friends followed close behind.

Mousey led everyone to the wizard's hut and squeezed under the door. The princess opened the door and gasped. Inside were piles of treasure that the wizard had been stealing from her!

"Guards, take the wizard and his cat away!" declared the princess. She turned to Dora and her friends. "Thank you for returning my ring. It is very special to me."

The princess gave Dora, Pablo, and Naiya gold medals as rewards. And she decided to keep Mousey as her royal pet!

"Thanks for breaking the spell," Pablo told his friends. "Now I'm big enough for story time for the kids!"

"I think we have a great story for them," Dora said with a smile. "The story of how we returned the ring and broke the spell together! *¡Todos juntos!*"